Jakers!™

Piggley Helps Out

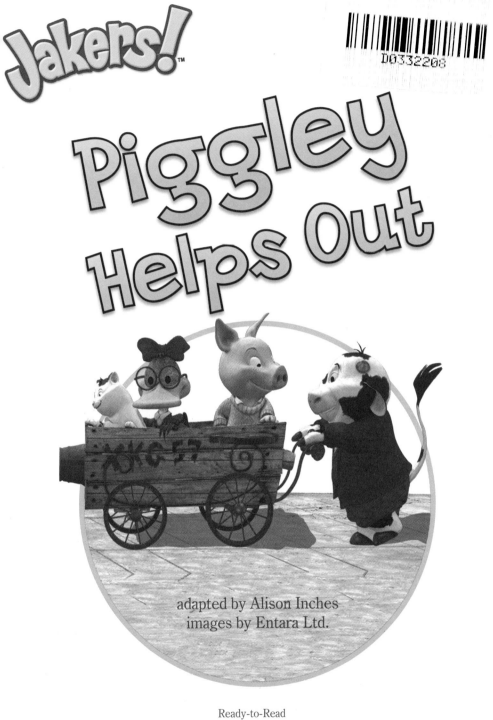

adapted by Alison Inches
images by Entara Ltd.

Ready-to-Read

Simon Spotlight
New York London Toronto Sydney

Based on the TV series *Jakers! The Adventures of Piggley Winks* created by Entara Ltd.

SIMON SPOTLIGHT
An imprint of Simon & Schuster Children's Publishing Division
1230 Avenue of the Americas, New York, New York 10020
SIMON SPOTLIGHT, READY-TO-READ, and colophon are registered trademarks of Simon & Schuster, Inc.
Manufactured in the United States of America
First Edition
2 4 6 8 10 9 7 5 3 1
Library of Congress Cataloging-in-Publication Data
Inches, Alison.
Piggley helps out / by Alison Inches.— 1st ed.
p. cm. — (Ready-to-read)
"Based on the TV series Jakers! The Adventures of Piggley Winks."
Summary: Piggley and his friends set out to find a missing cat that belongs to Miss Nanny.
ISBN-13: 978-0-689-87614-1 ISBN-10: 0-689-87614-9
[1. Cats—Fiction. 2. Lost and found possessions—Fiction. 3. Pigs—Fiction.] I. Title. II. Series.
PZ7.I355Pk 2005
[E]—dc22
2004010703

 is sad.

MISS NANNY

Her  is lost!

CAT

"We can find your !"

CAT

say , , and .

PIGGLEY   FERNY   DANNAN

"Thank you," says .
MISS NANNY

"If you can find my ,
CAT

I will give you ."
CANDY

"Jakers!" says .
PIGGLEY

"We **love** !"
CANDY

"Tell us about your ,"
CAT

says  .
DANNAN

"My  is white,"
CAT

says  .
MISS NANNY

"My  loves 🚗 rides,

CAT　　　　　CAR

🧺, and 🐟.

BASKETS　　　FISH

My 🐱 is the best 🐱

CAT　　　　　　CAT

in the 🌏."

WORLD

PIGGLEY   FERNY   DANNAN

look for the

CAT

all day long.

 **PIGGLEY** , **FERNY** , and **DANNAN** are

about to give up when . . .

"Look!" says .
DANNAN

"I see the 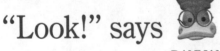!"
CAT

The 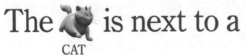 is next to a .
CAT   PLANT

,  , and

PIGGLEY   FERNY   DANNAN

put the  in their  .

CAT   WAGON

"  will be so happy!"

MISS NANNY

says  .

PIGGLEY

But it is not 's 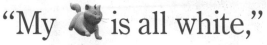!

MISS NANNY   CAT

"My 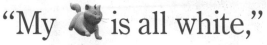 is all white,"

CAT

says .

MISS NANNY

 gives  ,

MISS NANNY   PIGGLEY   FERNY

and candy for trying.

DANNAN

" 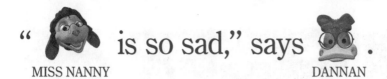 is so sad," says 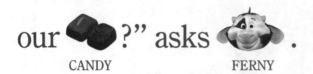 .

MISS NANNY   DANNAN

"How can we enjoy

our 🍬 ?" asks 🐮 .

CANDY   FERNY

"We **must** find her  !"
CAT

says  .
PIGGLEY

"What do we know about

MISS NANNY 's CAT ?" asks DANNAN.

" MISS NANNY 's CAT is all white,"

says PIGGLEY.

"She loves  rides,  ,
CAR   BASKETS

and  ," says  . "And
FISH   FERNY

she is the best  in the  ."
CAT   WORLD

"I know!" says  .
DANNAN

"The  is in the fish  !"
CAT   VAN

" 's is here!"

MISS NANNY   CAT

says  .

PIGGLEY

"Now we can take the

 home!"

CAT

"Not so fast!"

Who said that? It is !

HECTOR

"Give me the !" says .

CAT   HECTOR

"We will not give you

MISS NANNY's CAT," says PIGGLEY.

"But we will give you our CANDY."

HECTOR takes the CANDY.

, PIGGLEY FERNY, and DANNAN

take the CAT back to MISS NANNY.

"My CAT!" says MISS NANNY.

"I missed you so much!"

MISS NANNY thanks PIGGLEY ,

FERNY , and DANNAN

for their help.

"We made  happy!"

MISS NANNY

says .

PIGGLEY

"And that is better than

all the  in the !"

CANDY   WORLD